SHARING THE MOUNTA
THE THIRD

GW01453092

Copyright 2017 J.L Roberts
All rights reserved.

Table of Contents

Introduction

CHAPTER 1: Spring 1981

CHAPTER 2: Summer 1981

CHAPTER 3: Autumn 1981

CHAPTER 4: Winter 1981

Conclusion

Gallery

Introduction

There are many reasons to want to live atop of the Appalachian Mountains. The mountains are beautiful. To own a piece of the Appalachians is something to be proud of. From the bright early mornings with the birds singing and the whispers of the winds through the old grown trees to the beautiful sunsets in the evening and the fireflies at night illuminating the fields and the dense forests.

Jake and I bought a little part of the Appalachian Mountains which consisted of a farmhouse, barn, and eight acres of land. It was our paradise. We had planned on settling down and raising our children, along with farm animals, and to grow enough produce on the farm so that Jake could quit his job in the city and work on the farm full time.

This year would make our third year living on the farm. We were trying to raise our animals and grow our crops to sell to produce enough income to live happily in the mountains.

Being a city girl, it was tough living in the country trying to work on a farm. With the sounds of the countryside versus the city, it was hard to get used to.

As time went on, I got used to the strange sounds of the countryside. All but a few, which I don't think that anyone could get used to the sounds that an unknown creature makes.

Many strange and frightening occurrences went on in the year of 1981. It's much that it made it hard to try to get the daily chores finished. Not to mention that there was no relaxing on the back porch after a hard day's work.

Unfortunately, we did not make enough money from our crops from the last year for Jake to quit his job in the city. We were hoping that we could make it on the profits that the fields yielded, but, we would have to wait yet for another year for that to come to fruition.

Being left alone in the mountains when Jake had to go to work each week day, I felt very uncomfortable being alone at the farm with the children each day. But Jake had to make a living wage for us to live on and I had to do the daily chores. Life had to go on with us living on the farm. After all, it was our little paradise, and we put everything we had into the property, and we were not giving up on our dream. Not yet.

This year I was determined to make the best out of the situation we were in. I wanted to start enjoying life, our children, and the farm. We haven't had any odd occurrences in the first few months of 1981, and I knew that it would be a matter of time before our visitor may be back, but prayed that it wouldn't be back to terrorize us and our animals. As you read this book, it is obvious that my prayers would not be answered with this situation. The creature became braver, and we became more frightened. I was afraid to go out of the house if Jake was not there, and the children wanted to go out to play in the yard with their toys but I would not allow them to go out by themselves and they only stayed out for just a brief time each day.

This book is a continuation of the second book, "Sharing the Mountain with Bigfoot, the Second Year." If you haven't read the first and second book, please do because that's where it all started.

I will begin this book in the spring, just like the first and second book. It seemed that after the first snow fall of the first year, which was Christmas day, no odd occurrences happened until the spring. Looking back, that was when everything was peaceful, and my family had enjoyed the farm. We would go outside and play in the snow, and I didn't worry about anything except making sure my family was fed, and the chores were done. That brief time of the year was when I would fall in love with the farmhouse and the property all over again.

CHAPTER 1
SPRING 1981

The snow had melted away, and the spring flowers were sprouting out. The winds were blowing from the south, bringing the warmer weather with it and the sun was shining brightly through the windows of the farmhouse, warming the house and making the children excited to go outside to play in the yard.

Jake's parents, Arthur and Pearl, had gone back to their home after the first of the Year and Jake had to go back to work in the city, leaving me and the children at home alone once again. I missed the company of my in-laws and silently wished that they lived closer to us.

I went outside to the back porch and sat down in the rocking chair to enjoy my cup of coffee and admire the beauty of the trees starting to come alive. With the birds singing and the warm, gentle winds blowing around me, I felt wonderful. It was a beautiful day, and I knew the children would be out in a matter of minutes to play with their toys in the bright sunshine.   But before the children came out to join me on the back porch, I heard a car pulling up to the house in the front. I knew it wasn't Jake because he just left for his job in the city. However, due to the familiar sound of the car, I knew it was my neighbor and friend Karen coming for a social visit.

John and Karen were our neighbors, friends, and we considered them a part of our family. They also had been through a lot of dramatic and terrorizing encounters with the creature that had been lurking in the woods around our property and theirs, but it seemed that it did not affect Karen and John any longer. They had many dogs on their property for protection, and I thought that maybe we should do the same.

I got up and walked down the steps of the back porch and met Karen on the side of the house, as she made her way to the back as if she knew where I was.

"Isn't it a beautiful day?" Karen asked as she walked up to me and wrapped her arms around my neck.

"Yes, so beautiful" I replied, happy to see her while I embraced her hug.

As we turned and started walking back to the back porch, the children were coming out through the kitchen door onto the porch and made their way out into the yard. Karen and I watched as Emma wobbled to the sand box while Cody ran around the yard with a toy airplane in his hand while the toy holster and pistol dangled around on his hip.

Karen sat down in the rocker on the back porch while I went into the kitchen to refill my cup and poured Karen a fresh cup of coffee. Karen took the cup of coffee and lit a cigarette.

We started our visit with small talk of how everyone was doing and what we were going to plant in the gardens this year. Karen was telling me about her flowers that she was going to plant this year when she lit another cigarette.

I know Karen. When she started smoking, I knew something was worrying her.

"What's bothering you, Karen?" I asked as I watched her inhale the smoke from her cigarette.

"I hate to tell you this," Karen started as she blew the smoke out of her lungs and looked at me with sad eyes.

"We had a visitor last night at our farm" Karen finished in a lowered tone.

I stared at her for a moment trying to comprehend as to what she had said to me.

"What do you mean?" I asked, knowing what she meant but didn't want to believe it.

When she didn't answer, my heart started pounding harder, and my hands started shaking so bad that I had to put down my coffee mug on the table that was next to the rocker.

After tearing my gaze off Karen, I realized that I couldn't hear Cody playing in the yard close to the porch where we were sitting.

I started looking to see if I could see Cody in the back yard but he was nowhere in sight.

I jumped up to look to see where he was. As I was scanning the back yard, I saw him running toward the tree line at the back of the property.

My heart dropped to my stomach, and I panicked! I started running down the porch steps and through the field toward where Cody was. It was hard running through the freshly plowed field that Jake had plowed just a few days ago.

As Cody was getting closer to the tree line, my legs started to get weak, and I started yelling to Cody to stop and come back. He didn't stop!

As I got closer to Cody, I started to smell that same pungent odor that I had smelled before. Then I heard what sounded like something in the woods started running away from us and breaking everything in its path.

That made me run faster to Cody. I finally caught up with him, grabbed him up and started running back to the house with him in my arms.

I finally made it back to the house with Cody, and I noticed that Karen had Emma in the front living room waiting for us to come back.

I reached the front living room, sat Cody down on the sofa and collapsed into the chair that was close to the fire place.

My heart was racing, and my breathing was very labored. I sat there slumped in the chair trying to catch my breath when suddenly I realized that I did not lock the back door when I came through.

I jumped back up and ran to the back door and made sure it was locked.

As I was locking the back door, I looked out of the kitchen window. As I was staring out the window, I did not notice Karen had walked into the kitchen.

"Sweetheart, that may have been just a deer in the woods," Karen said as she sat down at the kitchen table.

I turned around to go sit down at the table with Karen.

"It sounded way too big to be just a deer," I said as I wiped sweat from my forehead.

"Did you see anything?" Karen replied.

"No, but I heard it, and I didn't want to take any chances of it being anything else," I said as I got up to get a drink of water.

Karen was right. It could have been a deer. I didn't see anything, and I just heard an animal in the woods and my imagination got the best of me. Especially when she just told me about their visitor at their farm the night before. But deer do not have a strong horrible odor to them either.

When Jake came home from work that evening, I told him about what Karen had told me and the incident with Cody.

I noticed Jake's facial and body language. His face went from smiling to a concerned look, and his body stiffened.

"I think I will try to put some traps out to see if that will deter the animals from coming close to the house," Jake said as he started towards the front door to go feed the animals.

That made me feel better. I didn't want to catch any animals in a trap, but if it would deter any wild animals from coming close to the farmhouse, I was ready to give it a try.

The weekend was here, and Jake didn't have to go to work. He was up early in the morning to feed the hogs, goats, and chickens and work in the fields preparing them for planting.

I had the chores finished, and I wanted to relax a little while out on the back porch.

It was a beautiful Saturday morning, and I wanted to enjoy it.

I sat on the back-porch steps watching the children play in the back yard, and I also watched Jake in the fields on his tractor. As I watched Jake on the tractor, I noticed that he kept looking at the tree line in the back of the property. It seemed that something was drawing his attention toward the woods. He plowed about half of the field when I noticed that he was headed to the barn to put the tractor away for the day. I thought of that as being a little bit odd, for Jake usually finished the fields when he would plow.

When Jake put the tractor into the barn, I watched as he walked toward the back of the house where the children and I were in the back yard. When he reached the step where I sat, he looked down at me and sighed.

"Are you ready to go into town?" He asked, looking at me with those big beautiful blue eyes but a worried look on his face.

I knew what he wanted to purchase from town. He had already mentioned that he wanted to get traps to go around the property to ward off wild animals from coming close to the house.

"I'll get the children ready," I said as I got up and called the children to come to me. I had the children cleaned and dressed in clean clothes, and we drove down our long driveway, headed toward town.

The drive down the mountain was a beautiful site. With the trees in bloom and the abundant wild flowers that lined the road, it would not take long for one to fall in love with the mountains. Jake and I sat in silence in the truck as we admired the beauty that surrounded us.

As we reached the town, the first place we stopped was the Co-op, the only place that may have traps for sale. Jake pulled up to the building and went inside while I stayed in the truck with the children. After about ten minutes, Jake came out of the store with a load of traps. He put them in the back of the truck, opened the driver side door, stepped in, started it and turned and looked at me. He knew I would ask him about the traps.

"They're bear traps," Jake said before I had time to ask him about them.

"Bear traps?" I asked, puzzled that we could buy bear traps at a Co-op.

"That's the only traps they had. It's the bear traps or nothing" Jake said as we pulled out of the parking lot and onto the main highway.

I was happy with that for I knew that having the bear traps was better than having nothing at all.

While we were in town, we needed to purchase some necessities that we were running low with. We stopped at the local market and shopped around for a while, then to the shoe store to buy the children new shoes. We also stopped at our favorite restaurant before we headed to the grocery store for the much-needed food to fill the cupboards.

We were having an enjoyable time, and I realized how much I missed the city. I took for granted the convenience the city had when we lived there and being around other people made me feel safe. I silently wished for that moment that we still lived in this small city.

After we had finished our shopping, it was time to leave and go back to our home that was perched in the mountains. But before we were ready to leave, the sky became dark and the rain started pouring down. It was raining so hard that the wipers on our truck were useless.

Jake pulled over to the side of the road to put a trap on the pile of groceries that we had in the back of the truck. When he got back into the truck, he was drenched. But that was the least of our problems. We had to drive up the mountain in one of the worst storms that we had had in a very long time.

We finally made it home safely, put the children to bed and the groceries into the cupboards and started to get ready to go to bed. I was exhausted from the day's activities and was ready for a good night's rest.

The storm raged on the whole night but luckily the children slept through it, and I had a restful night's sleep. The next day, the storm had passed, and the sun was shining once again.

Jake's main priority for the day was to put the traps out to surround the perimeter of the opening of the property, just inside the tree line. It was a daunting task, and it took him half a day to set them up. But after they were in place, I felt a little safer going out in the yard with the children.

The rest of the day was spent on the much-needed yard work and repairing things around the house. After that, we had a nice family dinner and relaxed on the back porch while we enjoyed our family time together with our children.

That night, after the children were in bed, and Jake in a deep sleep, it was hard for me to relax. I had many things running through my mind, and I could not go to sleep. But after a while, I started to doze off when suddenly, something startled me wide awake.

It was a long howl!! The same long guttural howl that I have heard before. It was not close to the house, but at that moment, I knew that our visitors were back!

The next morning, Jake had to go back to the city for his job. He arose early to feed the farm animals while I mustered up enough energy to get up and fix breakfast for him and the children. I was exhausted from not getting any sleep the night before after I heard the screams in the woods.

It didn't take long for Jake to come storming back into the house and headed for the phone in the front living room.

I couldn't help to notice the anger and fear that showed on his face and my heart started racing, knowing that something was very wrong.

The first phone call was to his job, telling them that he would not be in that day and explained a little why he was not going to be there. The second phone call was to our neighbor John.

After Jake had hung up the phone, I had to know what was going on.

"The hog pen is destroyed, and all the hogs are gone," Jake said in an angry voice, as he stood up and ran his fingers through his hair.

"What? No!" I said as an over whelming feeling of fear crept over me.

"John is coming over to see what can be done about this creature," Jake said as he walked closer to the front door, retrieved his shotgun and started loading it with bullets.

"Is Karen coming over too? I asked, not wanting to stay at the house alone.

"I'm sure she will" Jake replied.

I felt a little relief knowing that Karen would be here at the house with me while the men will be out in the woods to find a solution to our problem.

John and Karen arrived, and the men prepared to go into the woods for the day. Karen and I watched from the kitchen windows as they walked behind the house to the tree line and into the woods.

I turned to Karen and saw the worried expression on her face, my hands started shaking, and the tears started rolling down my face. I sat down at the kitchen table and wept.

Later that evening the men came back from their adventure in the woods. They had gone to the cave that they found before, and it was abandoned. They were surprised that they did not find bones in as they did before. The men roamed around in the woods and found some structures that looked to be big nests. They tore the structures down when they saw them, hoping that would deter the animals from staying around this area. Sadly, it did not work out the way we hoped.

That night as Jake and I were going to bed, I heard Emma rustling around in her crib and then she started crying and called for me. Before I could walk to her bedroom, she was crying hysterically. I rushed to her crib to pick her up and calm her down. Emma kept pointing to the window and crying. I started walking toward the window when suddenly, a small pebble hit the window. I Panicked!

I ran out of the bedroom with Emma in my arms, headed to the master bedroom where Jake was lying on the bed. He jumped up when he saw me with Emma.

"What's wrong with her?" Jake asked as he gets up from the bed.

"There's something throwing pebbles at Emma's bedroom window!" I screamed in a hysterical voice.

Jake hurriedly grabbed his rifle that was in the closet and rushed to Emma's bedroom window while I followed and stood in the doorway. That's when I saw four glowing red eyes that were looking up toward where Jake was standing.

Jake aimed the rifle toward the red eyes and stood there, looking through the scope.

I closed my eyes and waited for the rifle to fire, but it never happened. I opened my eyes only to see Jake in the same position as he was. He had not moved a muscle! He looked to be in a trance!

I ran over to where he was standing and grabbed his arm.

"Jake!" I screamed in his ear.

Jake jumped as if I scared him and he came out of the trance. He then put the rifle down and hurriedly closed the bedroom window.

I was trembling while I watched Jake close the window. He then turned and looked straight into my eyes, and I saw the fear in my husband's eyes. I knew he was slowly breaking down.

Suddenly, as if out of a horror movie, a flash of lightning lit up Emma's bedroom and the thunder was so loud that it shook the windows. The rain started pouring down making it hard to hear in the house.

We made our way back into the master bedroom with both children in the bed with us. I was trying to get comfortable and tried to get a little sleep. But with the terrorizing activity that went on that day, the lightning and loud thunder, there was no sleep to be had.

The next day, in fear of losing his job, Jake had to go to the city to work at his job. I knew he did not want to leave us at the house alone, but I assured him that we would be safe and that I knew how to use a weapon if I had to. As he was getting ready for work, I wanted to ask him why he did not shoot at the creatures with the red glowing eyes last night, but I also knew he was exhausted and had to work. He would tell me in his own time. I just had to wait.

The rain continued for days, and I was getting behind on the chores that had to be done. Our farm animals were dwindling down to only goats and a few chickens, and we did not have anything planted in the fields.

I could tell that Jake was getting anxious about the fields and disgusted about the few animals that we had left. He had worked so hard to get the farm going in this year, but the weather was not on his side.

"If the rains don't stop, we will not have anything planted this year" Jake blurted out as he looked out of the kitchen windows at the plowed, bare fields.

"I know honey, and it will be too late for planting before long" I replied, as I wrapped my arms around his waist and looked out toward the back field.

We turned to go into the living room, and Jake turned on the television to watch the local weather before he had to drive down the mountain to his job.

To my dismay, the rain would not stop for a while, but when it did stop, it wasn't long before another storm would hit.

There was one advantage about it raining every day. I noticed that when it rained, we had no visitor from the woods and no odd occurrences with the farm animals. In some ways, it was peaceful, and I would relax a little while I watched the storm clouds roll by.

A couple of weeks went by, and the storms would come and go, then come back again. The yard and fields were flooded, making them into ponds and the planting season had come to an end. That meant that we would not have anything to sell in the fall and Jake would have to stay at his job in the city for yet another year. It seemed that we were losing hope with our little paradise.

But we were not going to give up on this farm. We had worked so hard and put our life savings into it that we had no option but to make it work.

CHAPTER 2

SUMMER 1981

The summer months were here, and the humidity came along with them. It continued to rain off and on for the first part of the summer. This year was the rainiest summer months that I have ever witnessed, and it made the children stay indoors. Cody and Emma, nor I was happy with that.

Since we had no crops to tend to and only a few animals to feed, Jake's chores were not as hard on him every morning and evening. He also had a little more time to tend to Max. Jake enjoyed riding Max and more often, I would find him in the barn with our horse.

It was the weekend, and Jake was out in the barn with Max. Since the rain had quit and the sun started peeking out from behind the dark clouds, I took advantage of the opportunity and hung a few items of laundry on the line to dry.

The ground was still soggy from all the rains that we had from the day before, and I carefully made my way to the line. When I got half way to the clothes line, carrying a basket full of wet clothes, I noticed the mud puddles that I needed to avoid stepping in.

I came upon one mud puddle, and something did not look normal. I stopped and looked a little closer, and suddenly I knew what I was looking at.

A footprint! As I started to look around the muddy yard, I noticed there were more footprints. I put the basket of clothes down and decided to follow the footprints.

I noticed that they were pointing to the front of the house. I started to walk beside them and followed them to the front of the house. When I reached the front porch, I noticed that the prints kept going around to the side of the house.

I kept following the print until they came to an erupt stop. Right below Emma's bedroom!

My heart started racing as I looked up to Emma's bedroom window and noticed that the prints were facing the house.

As I studied the footprints, I started to get an overwhelming feeling of being watched. As I stood there facing the house, I became frightened and did not want to turn around to see if anything was behind me in the woods. I was frozen in my tracks, staring at the house!

Just when I had the nerve to turn around to peer into the woods, I heard a deep growl that came from behind me. Terror gripped at my soul, and my blood ran down to my feet. My legs became weak as a chill ran up my spine.

With my heart beat pounding in my ears, I finally started to run toward the front of the house. It seemed to take a long time to reach the front porch, but as I came to the front, I kept running toward the barn where Jake and the children were.

As I reached the barn door, I ran into Jake.

"Whoa, careful now," Jake said as he caught me in his arms and stopped me in a full run.

I tried to tell Jake what I just went through but the words were not coming out right. I was talking so fast that Jake could not understand me. That made me more anxious and frustrated.

While trying to tell Jake what I had witnessed, we were all suddenly startled by a loud scream that echoed through the woods, and it came from the same direction on the other side of the house where I just came from.

Jake stepped in front of me and walked out of the barn door with his weapon drawn. I picked Emma up on my hip and took Cody's hand and followed Jake out of the barn.

As we passed the clothes line, I thought about picking up the laundry basket and taking it back inside the house. But I had Emma in my arms, and the wet clothes that were left in the basket were the least of my worries.

As I brought the children into the safety of the house, I prayed that Jake would be safe and maybe put an end to the terror that was now so close to the house.

When I did not hear any gun shots ring out, my mind started to race, and the thoughts were giving me more concern.

"What if the creature lured Jake away from the house, or worse what if it attacked him" was running through my mind.

My anxiety was so great that I ran to the front door and opened it, stepped onto the front porch and peered around to the side of the house.

As soon as I was looking around the house, I heard someone walking in the woods.

Jake emerged from the woods, and I felt a sudden relief pour over me. But when I saw Jake's concerned look on his face, the fear crept back, and I had to know what was going on.

"Thank God you're back," I said as I ran down the steps and met him coming out of the woods.

"Go back into the house, Jada" Jake said in an authoritative but protective voice.

I obeyed Jake and turned to go back into the house. I noticed that while I walked back up the steps, Jake followed me into the front living room.

While Jake tried to relax in the front room of the house, and the children played with their toys on the floor, I started to prepare for the evening meal. I had the curtains in the kitchen window drawn, but whenever I would hear a noise coming from outside, my heart would skip a beat and a pang would go through my stomach. Mostly, the noises that I would hear would come from the few chickens that we had left, roaming in the yard.

After dinner, Jake went to feed the animals. He left the house with his shotgun in tow, and when he came back, he looked a little relieved that nothing was out of place.

After the children were bathed and put to bed, it was time to retire to my own bed. I was exhausted, but I knew that I would not get the rest that I needed.

A couple of weeks went by with no trace of our visitors from the woods. I started to let my guard down a little and the children needed to go outside to play in the yard and get a little fresh air. I also needed to finish the laundry that I had gotten behind on. I would not go to the laundry line without a weapon of some sort by my side, and I would scan the area before I took a step outside.

When I thought it was safe, I would go outside to the line with a basket full of wet clothes to hang in the sun. I noticed how beautiful the day was. The sun was shining brightly, the birds were singing their beautiful songs, and the westward winds made the day with a cool breeze. But at the time, I didn't know that the cool winds were from a brutal storm that was headed our way.

After the children and I had enjoyed the day out in the back yard, the winds started to pick up, and the dark clouds started to roll in. The sky became dark, and I could hear the thunder rumbling in the distance.

"It's time to go into the house," I said to Cody and Emma as they continued playing with their toys.

Cody and Emma were reluctant to come into the house when I called, but when the rains hit them, they started running to get on the porch, into the house and into the kitchen, where they waited to be fed.

As I was feeding the children, I noticed that the storm was getting worse. I started to worry about Jake driving up the mountain in the storm, and I silently prayed for his safety.

As the storm progressed, the harder the rains fell, the fierce lightning became almost constant, and the thunder rattled all the windows in the house. The gale force winds were whipping the trees so much that they looked to break at any moment.

I took the children to the front room of the house where the television was located. I turned it on to try to calm the children, and as soon as I pushed the button, the electricity flickered and then went dark.

Between trying to find candles for light and trying to calm two small children that were naturally frightened by the storm, my anxiety began to rise once again.

After I found the candles and calmed the children, we snuggled on the sofa waiting for the lights to flicker back on. It seemed but a little time had passed when we heard Jake pulling up to the house in the truck. By the time he opened the front door, he was drenched.

After a good laugh at Jake standing in the doorway, drenched to the bone, I helped him take off the wet clothes and replaced them with his favorite robe that he liked to lounge around the house with.

After dinner, which consisted of sandwiches and potato chips, we relaxed in the front room. We watched as the candles cast shadows on the wall and we listened to the storm that was raging on and on.

The next day, the storm had passed, and the sun started to peek through the clouds. The birds were singing once again, and the electricity had come back to life during the night.

I arose early to go to the kitchen to prepare breakfast for Jake and the children. I opened the kitchen window curtains to let the natural light in. I looked out of the window and noticed that the barn door had been opened.

Jake had to go out in the storm the night before to feed the animals and tend to Max. I thought that maybe he forgot to close the barn door in his hurried state to get the chore done and to return to the warm, dry house.

As I stared out of the window, I heard Jake walking into the kitchen, headed toward me.

"Did you forget to close the barn door last night?" I asked as I stared out of the window toward the barn.

"No, I didn't" Jake replied as he looked over my shoulder and out toward the barn.

"Damn it," Jake said in a lowered voice as he turned and walked to the back door and toward the barn.

I continued with breakfast when I realized that Jake was back into the kitchen and headed for the shotgun that was by the front door.

"Where are you going? I asked, startled that he was checking the shotgun to see if it was loaded with bullets while he walked passed me, headed to the back door.

"Max is not in the barn. I have to find him" Jake replied as he walked down the steps and toward the tree line in the back of the property.

I watched from the back porch as Jake scanned the bare muddy fields for Max's prints. Then I watched as he disappeared into the thick woods, not to be seen until later that afternoon.

When muddy, hungry, and aggravated Jake came back from the woods, he told me what he had discovered and my heart sunk.

Jake had found Max in the worse viable way for a horse to be. Max was lying on his side with two broken legs and unable to move. He was suffering in the state he was in, and Jake could not bring him out of the woods.

Sadly, Max was no more. Jake had laid him to rest in the thick woods behind our property.

As I watched Jake tell me what had happened to Max, I knew it had affected him greatly. He had bonded with our beloved horse, and the loss of Max would affect the whole family. Especially Cody.

It was very hard to tell the children about Max. I knew that the children loved him and thought that he was family. But after telling them, I was surprised at how Cody reacted to the news. For a child, not yet five years old, he took the news of Max better than I had thought.

A few days went by, and I had to prepare for a birthday. Emma was turning three years old, and I was getting things together to celebrate her special day.

The county fair was being held in town the weekend before her birthdate, and I thought that would be a good place to go for her birthday surprise. I also needed a break from the farm, and I was longing to see the town and be around other people.

Jake and I gathered the children and drove down the mountain to the city. I was excited to see the bustling small town and all it had to offer. From the busy four lane road that went down the middle of the town, to the small one owner shops that lined the streets, and the many people walking the sidewalks between the shops with their purchases in hand or dangling from bags around their wrists.

The town was so close to the Appalachian Mountains that it became a tourist town. In the summer months, the town was bursting at the seams with tourist, making the traffic unbearable for the residents of the small city.

When Jake and I lived in the city, I would dread the summer tourist months. It was a living nightmare to drive from work to home, and I would curse every minute when I was stuck in traffic. But living in the mountains with no one around, I started to enjoy going into town and to be around all the people.

We finally made our way to the county fair. The children were overjoyed to see the small rides and all the things made for children to enjoy.

We stocked up on all the fried foods and sweet cakes, candies and caramel apples that we could handle. The children rode all the rides that they were allowed on, and Jake and I would try to find the shady spots that were offered. Mainly the shade of any tree that we could find.

As the day turned into night, it was time to leave the fair and drive home. With our sunburned skin and our bellies full of junk food, we headed up the mountain toward home. The exhausted children fell asleep on the long drive up the mountain, and I couldn't wait to retire to my bed as soon as we returned to the house. I was in need of a good night's rest.

The following day, after a peaceful night's sleep, I was in a joyous mood. I arose early and started my chores to get them done early in the day, so I would have time to relax in the afternoon. I started cleaning the kitchen and washing the morning dishes when the phone in the other room started to ring.

When I answered the phone, it didn't take long to recognize the familiar voice that filled my ear. It was Karen. I enjoyed talking to Karen when she would call or come over for a visit. We had so much in common, and she understood my feelings of being a city girl trying to live comfortably in the countryside.

I sat down in the chair that was closest to the phone and knew that when Karen called it was time to take a break and we would have an extended conversation. Our conversation consisted of the normal greetings, and the "I hope everyone is doing well" lines. I was enjoying our conservation when suddenly Karen became quiet.

I didn't have time to ask her any questions when suddenly she began talking again.

"We had another visitor last night at our house, Jada," Karen said, taking a pause and waited for me to respond.

As I sat there with the phone perched to my ear, I tried to comprehend what Karen had revealed to me.

But before I had a chance to reply, Karen started to tell me about the activities that happened around their farm the night before.

"It all started about 9 pm last night. The dogs started barking, and I could hear noises around our barn. John stepped out of the house with his shotgun to investigate. What he found was the barn was ransacked. But before it had time to do any more damage, our dogs must have ran it off. I think the creature was trying to attack our livestock because they are easy targets."

As Karen was telling her story of what happened the night before, at their farm, a feeling of dread washed over me. I felt frightened once again and wanted to make sure that the doors were locked and we were safe in the house.

As I was sitting in the front of the house listening to Karen talk on the phone, I heard Cody running in the kitchen and making his way toward to me. While I was talking to Karen, I didn't notice that he had gone outside the back yard to retrieve a toy that he had left near the porch.

"Mommy, there's a big monster in the yard out there," he said, as he looked at me with wide eyes and an excited tone in his voice, as he pointed toward the back of the house.

As soon as Cody said those words, I dropped the phone and rushed out to the back porch to see what Cody was talking about.

As I scanned the back of the property, I saw a black figure running toward the tree line in the back of the property.

I panicked! I ran back into the kitchen, closed and locked the door. I peered out the kitchen window to make sure that the creature had left.

When I couldn't see anything out in the woods, I remembered that I did not hang the receiver up on the base on the phone. I rushed to the receiver that was lying on the floor and was surprised that Karen was still there on the phone.

When I heard Karen's voice, I started to tell her about what had just happened.

It didn't take long before I heard Karen's car driving up the driveway and pulling up to the house.

I felt relieved when I saw her walking up the front porch steps. What a wonderful friend Karen was to me. I knew that she had a busy day with her chores, and she took the time to come over to comfort me and stayed until Jake came home from work. I am forever grateful.

That night while I was getting ready for bed, I silently said a prayer for strength and the courage to stay in the woods when Jake wasn't here to protect me and the children. I also prayed that we wouldn't have any more problems with the Bigfoot that were roaming the mountains around the area. For I knew that I could not take much more of this. I needed a miracle.

Little did I know that our nightmare just began.

CHAPTER 3
AUTUMN 1981

The best part of living in the
Appalachian Mountains are the seasons.
Autumn had always been my favorite season
while we ... the farmhouse. The
weather had been hot and humid in the last
part of the summer months, and I was ready
for the change. From the trees with their
...nt colored leaves of red, orange, and
yellow, to the cool breezes that blew from
the north. I was ready to enjoy the pleasures
that autumn would bring.

... the rains from spring and early
summer had ruined our crops, we did not
have anything to harvest or sell during the
autumn. That meant that Jake had to keep
working at his job in the city.

That made me very frustrated. My hope
... to be producing enough ...
quit his job and I thought

by the third year, that we would have the farm established.

I was woken when I heard the children playing in the downstairs front living room. I also realized that Jake had been out of the bed for a while when I reached over to where he would lie, and it was cool. I knew he was down stairs with the children when I arose slowly and started walking toward the stairs.

I followed the cheerful laughter and squeals from the children and came to where they were. When I reached the front living room, I noticed that Cody, Emma, and Jake were on the front room floor spending quality time with each other. More likely, wrestling with each other.

I silently walked passed them for not wanting to interrupt their rough housing time together and went into the kitchen for a fresh cup of coffee.

I sat down at the kitchen table with my cup of coffee and watched Jake and the children play together. I admired Jake for taking the time out of his busy schedule to spend time with Cody and Emma.

As I started to prepare breakfast, Jake stopped playing on the floor and walked into the kitchen.

He came up from behind me and put his arms around my waist and gave me a hug.

"Let's go to town for breakfast," Jake said as he kissed my cheek and hugged me tighter.

That made me happy. I would never pass up the chance to go into town.

"I'll get the children ready to go," I said as I rushed up to the second floor to put on different clothes and made sure the children were ready.

We headed down the mountain to the small bustling city. We stopped at our favorite diner to have our breakfast.

While we were there, we shopped in the small shops that were located around town. I picked out a few fall decorations to go on the front porch thinking that maybe it would change the mood that I was in about the farmhouse.

We had a wonderful time shopping in town, and we took the children to the city park to get the much-needed exercise and outdoor activities that we hadn't had the chance to have in a long time.

The afternoon had come and gone and the evening was fast approaching. We had our dinner in town at a southern buffet style diner that was another one of our favorite restaurants in the city.

After the long day in the overcrowded city, it was time to go back into the mountains. I secretly wished that we were still living in our little-rented house that we left three years ago to go live in our paradise in the mountains.

The drive up the mountain was a peaceful one. The children were exhausted and slept all the way to the farmhouse. Nightfall was upon us as we pulled into the driveway and I could hardly wait until I was in the house so I could relax from the day's activities.

I put the children to bed and went back down to the front living room to watch the local news with Jake. As I was sitting down on the sofa, something caught my attention that was blaring out of the television set.

"A strange encounter happened earlier today in the mountains where a family was terrorized by an animal that came into their campsite," the local newswoman said as she stared at me from the television set.

I stared back at the woman that was inside the box that was in our front living room. With my mouth agape and my eyes glued to her, I listened to every word that came out of her mouth.

I was stunned to hear that a family that was on a camping trip in a well-known state park that was nestled in the mountains were terrorized by an unknown creature in broad daylight.

The state park was not close to our property, and I started to think that either the Bigfoot that had been around our property traveled for long distances, or there was more than what we thought to be around.

My mind started racing and the questions that I knew that no one could answer started swirling around in my head. As I was in deep thought, Jake suddenly brought me back to reality.

"If that is the same thing that has been around here, maybe they are moving away from this area," Jake said as he looked at me with a grin, knowing that his words would calm me.

After hearing that, it did calm my nerves a little. I started thinking that maybe Jake was correct and the creature was moving away from our farm, and my hope of living in our little paradise peacefully came back to me.

That night as Jake and I retired to bed, I fell into a deep sleep and had the much-needed rest that I had in a long time.

The next morning, I woke refreshed and ready to face the day. After breakfast, I took the children out to the front porch to put up the décor that we had purchased the day before.

The weather was perfect. With the cool breeze that blew through the dry leaves that were barely hanging on the trees and the smell of autumn all around us, I had a renewed love for our farm.

I started decorating the porch with pumpkins, and I perched the cornstalks on the side of the porch by the flower garden. While I was helping Emma with her little pumpkin, putting it on the side of the one of the step leading up to the porch, when suddenly, something caught my eye that was close to the driveway.

I started looking down the driveway, and I noticed that one of the trees were moving more than the other trees. When I looked closer, I noticed that something was in the tree.

As I was staring at the object that was in the tree, I suddenly realized what I was looking at.

A small ape-like creature was staring back at me! A juvenile Bigfoot!

My heart started pounding, and a chill went up to my spine! I hurriedly gathered Cody and Emma, and we ran up the steps, as I reached the porch, I turned to look back to where I saw the creature, but to my surprise, it was gone.

As soon as I shut the front door, I heard Jake coming into the kitchen from the back door. He turned his attention to me as I was waving my hand for him to come quickly.

As he approached, he opened the front door and looked out.

"What am I supposed to be looking at honey," Jake said as he looked out the front door.

"Do you see it?" I asked in a low panicked voice.

Jake shrugged his shoulders sarcastically, said that our decorations looked nice on the front porch. He then closed the door and started walking back to the kitchen.

I followed him into the kitchen and explained to him what I saw in the tree.

"Are you sure you saw that?" Jake asked as he pulled an alcoholic beverage from the ice box, twisted the lid off and took a long drink from the bottle.

"Yes, I know what I saw," I said in an aggravated tone, knowing that Jake did not trust what I was telling him.

After a while, I started to think about what I had seen in the trees. Did I really see that or was it just my imagination? I started to doubt it myself. But I saw it in plain sight and in the bright sunlight. I knew that there was a creature in the tree that day.

The next day I was still a little nervous about the sighting that I had the day before. Jake had to go to work early in the morning and had my daily chores that I had to finish.

What really worried me was that if I saw a juvenile animal in the woods, there was a big chance that the mother would be close by also. That's what troubled me the most.

I managed to finish the laundry and had a few clothes hung on the line to dry. I took the children out to play in the back yard for a little while as I sat on the back-porch steps and watched them closely.

I would scan the area for any movement of any kind while the children played the yard.

While I looked down toward the open fields, where the weeds were growing, and a few corn stalks had sprouted up, I noticed something strange.

I haven't seen any deer in the fields all summer or fall. To think back, I haven't seen any deer all year.

Remembering back to the last two years since purchasing the property, the deer were in abundance around the farm.

Especially when driving up the mountain, we were guaranteed an appearance of a deer crossing the road. I do not remember the last time that we have had that experience.

That evening at dinner, I wanted to ask Jake about what he thought about the disappearing deer.

"Have you seen any deer lately? I asked.

Jake gave me a puzzled look, took a sip of his drink, and looked down at his plate of food as if he was thinking.

"I haven't thought about it, but no, I have not seen any deer lately," Jake said as he picked up his fork for another bite of food.

"It's strange" I replied as I dipped the spoon into the casserole dish to fill Emma's plate.

We finished our dinner with talking about other things. Jake would tell me about the things that would happen at his job and the rumors that were going around in town.

That made me miss the social gatherings that I would enjoy when we lived in the rented house in the city.

After dinner, Jake would go out to tend to the animals while I bathed the children and prepared them for bed.

When the kitchen was cleaned, and the children were asleep in their beds, I was ready to lie down for the night and sleep.

A few weeks had gone by, and surprisingly, everything was quiet and peaceful around the farm. There were no odd occurrences that happened, and I started to enjoy the mountain again.

As the weather was turning cooler, I enjoyed opening the windows for the cool breeze to blow through the house. What I liked the most when the temperature was changing were the cool nights that made sleeping under a blanket very enjoyable.

While I had finished pinning the last article of clothing on the line to dry, I thought of how nice it would be to have something grilled for dinner.

I checked the charcoal grill that was stationed on the back porch and thought that I could find something from the ice box to grill. I knew that Jake would be happy to have a nice dinner waiting for him when he returned from his job.

After I prepared the meat that I wanted to grill and started the grill, the smell of the grilled food was amazing, and I knew that Jake would be pleased with dinner that night.

After dinner, Jake and I went to sit on the back porch to relax and watch the children play in the yard before dark. The grill had cooled, but the smell of the freshly grilled food was lingering in the breeze.

"I hope that smell doesn't attract any animals to come close to the house" Jake blurted out as he looked toward the woods.

I never thought about that. Being a city girl, how did I know that I would attract carnivores from the woods to our house.

As I started to look around the back yard and into the woods, I silently wished I had thought of what Jake had just mentioned, and in my mind, and from that moment, I had vowed never to use the outside grill again.

That night when the children were asleep, I finished cleaning the kitchen, I headed up the stairs to our bedroom. I felt very tired, and I was ready for bed.

As soon as I crawled into bed, I realized that the room was a little warm and I wanted the cool night air to flow into the bedroom. I opened the window, returned to bed and retired into my pillow.

The breeze from the open window felt amazing. I thought to myself that I would get the best sleep as I sunk my head into the pillow and drifted off to sleep.

Later that night I was startled awake. At first, I didn't know what had woken me.

As I looked around the room to see if one of the children had come into the room, I realized everything in the house was quiet.

I tried to go back to sleep again, but as soon as my eyes closed, I suddenly heard the loudest scream coming through the opened window!

My eyes immediately opened, and I watched as Jake jumped straight up in bed. His eyes were wide open, and his breathing became labored as he sat there stunned.

"What was that?" I asked in a shaky voice as I looked at Jake.

Jake was about to answer my question when suddenly, another scream came through the opened window.

Jake pulled the covers off him, jumped up out of bed and headed toward the closet for his rifle.

My heart started pounding, but I couldn't move! I was in shock! All I could do was watch as Jake started loading the rifle.

Suddenly, I heard Emma crying from her bedroom, and I saw Cody running into our bedroom.

As I jumped out of bed and ran toward Emma, Cody ran passed me and jumped onto our bed and threw the covers over his head.

As I rushed back to the master bedroom with Emma in my arms, I noticed that Jake was still at the window with the rifle pointed out toward the woods.

"Do you see anything?" I asked in a quiet whisper.

"No" was the only word that Jake mumbled as he stared out the window.

I sat Emma on the bed and turned my attention back to Jake. I watched his every move and prayed that he would not see anything out in the yard close to the house.

Finally, Jakes tensed body relaxed a little, and he lowered the rifle from the window. He turned and walked around to the far side of the bed and leaned the rifle against the wall within reach.

As he climbed into bed, I noticed the fear and concern on his face and that worried me greatly.

I returned to the cramped bed to try to get some rest. But with the children in bed with us and the small space that was left for me to lie down in, I knew there would not be any sleep for the rest of the night.

The next day Jake arose early and went out in the woods behind our house. He wanted to investigate the surrounding area from where we had heard the screams from the night before. He also wanted answers for what had been lurking the woods around our house, and he was determined to find a solution to our problems.

I had great anxiety while Jake was in the woods. I kept blaming myself for the grilling that I had done the day before. I thought that for me cooking outdoors may have brought the creature around the house again and I started to feel frightened and unsafe once again.

While I waited on Jake to come out of the woods and for the much-needed answers that I so much longed for, I started to see movement right inside of the tree line.

My heart started to beat faster, and I started to shake. When the movement finally moved out of the woods and into the opening of the fields, I realized it was Jake, and I felt an instant relief.

As I watched him walk toward the house, I noticed that he was carrying an odd object. But as he approached the back porch I realized what that object was.

The bear traps. I had forgotten that Jake had put the bear traps around the property and I was shocked to see Jake carrying one up to the house.

"Looks like something had stepped on the bear trap," Jake said as he walked up the steps and onto the porch.

As I looked at the bear trap, I noticed that there was blood stains and hair still on the claws of the trap.

"Was it a bear? I asked as I studied the trap.

"I don't think so Jada" Jake replied.

"That scream last night was not a bear," Jake said as he laid the trap down on the back porch and ran his fingers through his hair and sighed.

He was right. The scream that we heard last night wasn't a bear's scream. I was hoping that the bear traps may have scared the creatures away from our farm. Unfortunately, I was wrong.

After telling Jake that my hope was that after last night, the creature might leave the area since the trap had injured it, we will never have to deal with it again.

"We can only hope, darling" Jake said after I told him my thoughts.

To my horrifying disbelief, the activity only increased after the trap incident. Our once beautiful paradise became a living nightmare. I didn't know how much more I could take. I loved my farmhouse, but what could Jake and I do about the visitors from the woods.

CHAPTER 4
WINTER 1981

Winter had finally arrived. With the cold winds that whipped the last remaining leaves off the trees and the threat of snow on the horizon, I was becoming excited about the holidays that would here before we knew it.

I would think back at the last couple years when winter was here, and I remembered that we did not have any weird activity around the farm in the winter.

Since Jake did not have any fields to harvest during the fall months, he spent his time on replenishing the firewood for the winter months. We had an abundance of firewood, and I could rest assured that we would stay nice and cozy all winter long.

The days were getting shorter and the nights were getting colder, but that didn't bother me for I enjoyed the quality family time in front of the beautiful fireplace that was in the front room of the house.

What did worry me was I would hear yells and screams on a nightly basis coming from the woods that surrounded the property.

I would have a dreadful feeling every night as I retired to bed. I knew that during the night that I would hear something strange coming from the woods. And for that, I was losing sleep.

Jake had acquired vacation days from his job, and he wanted to take them around the winter holidays. That made me happy for I knew he would be here with me and the children and I felt safe enough to go outside to finish my chores and allow the children to play in the yard.

Thanksgiving came and went with a breeze. I wished that we had family and friends over for the feast, but the only friends we had were John and Karen. But they had their own Thanksgiving at their place as their grown children came to visit them. But we had an enjoyable time, just Jake and I and the children. After Thanksgiving, I started preparing for another special day.

Cody's birthday was coming up, and I started to prepare for his birthday party. With him turning five years old, we had started preparing him for his first year of school that started in the next year. He was also excited about going to school and being around children his own age.

Even though I was exhausted from lack of sleep, we made the best of Cody's birthday party. We invited John and Karen over and had a very nice dinner with a cake made with Cody's favorite toppings.

After the party, we continued our social gathering in the living room in front of the fireplace, while the children played with their toys in their rooms.

As the night carried on, Jake and I shared our news about the creature from the woods to our neighbors.

As they listened to our stories, I watched as John and Karen listened to Jake as he told them what had been happening, I noticed how uncomfortable they became.

When Jake finished telling them about the activities that were happening around our property, I was stunned when they had their own story to tell.

"We understand what you are going through," Karen said right after Jake had finished telling them about the activities that were happening around the house.

"We have had a lot of activity around our place too" John continued after Karen.

"The barn had been ransacked, the farm animals have been disappearing, and our dogs are now scared to go out into the yard," Karen said as she shook her head in disbelief.

I was stunned at what John and Karen were telling us. It seemed to me that the creature was getting braver and coming around more often.

We were enjoying our ongoing visit with our neighbors while sitting in front of the fireplace when suddenly we heard a loud thump. Something hit the side of the house.

We were all startled. Jake and John jumped to their feet and rushed to the front door. With their handguns drawn, they went out to the front porch and down the steps to see what had hit the house.

As they rounded the house, Jake noticed that a piece of firewood was lying near the house, right below where it hit the house.

The men searched the surrounding area to see if they could spot anything out in the woods that could have thrown the piece of firewood, but they found no trace of the guilty culprit who was responsible for the deed.

It was getting late in the night, and John and Karen were ready to leave to go back to their home. We said our goodbye's and I watched as they drove down our long driveway until their tail lights faded into the darkness of the woods. Jake and I returned to the house, and I made sure that the front door was locked and secured for the night.

I was feeling exhausted, and I couldn't wait to crawl into bed for a much-needed rest.

The next morning, I woke up feeling weak and drained. After I had managed to pull myself out of bed, I realized that my head was pounding, my sinuses were clogged, and my ears felt blocked. I then diagnosed myself as having a head cold, and I felt miserable.

But life had to go on, the children had to be tended to, and the chores didn't magically disappear when I was sick. I had to be strong and try my best to overcome this dreadful sickness.

A very long, slow and miserable week had passed, and I started to feel better. I started to get into the holiday spirit, and I knew it was time to start with the Christmas décor and much anticipated Christmas shopping for the children.

While I was in a joyous mood, I wanted to get started on the decorations. I remembered that I had stashed all the Christmas décor that I used the previous year in the attic of the farmhouse.

With the help of Jake, Cody, and Emma, we had all the decorations out of the attic and onto the floor in the front of the house. We had an enjoyable time trying to put together all the lights, wreaths, and other décors on the outside of the house as well as on the walls of the fireplace.

Jake had nailed a string of flashing colored Christmas lights to the top of the porch that trailed down the pillars that ended at the hand rails of the steps.

After we had finished decorating the front of the house and had put all the décor up on the walls, we noticed that there was one important thing that was missing. The Christmas tree.

Remembering back from the previous year when we had gone out into the woods to find a Christmas tree and cut it down ourselves. I knew that this year would be different. I was a little weary of going out into the woods in search of a tree, so instead, we went and purchased a tree from a vendor in town.

It was getting later in the evening after we had finished putting the decorations up and around the house, but the children were not happy until we had a Christmas tree. I agreed with them. With all the challenging work that had been done, it seemed to be incomplete without a lit tree in the bay window. It was time to go to town.

We all jumped into the truck and headed down the mountain and into the well-lit town. The townspeople were in the process of putting up the decorations that were used each year around the small town, and I could feel the spirit of Christmas coming to life as we drove to our tree farm destination.

As we pulled into the parking space of the tree farm, I was a little overwhelmed from all the cut trees that we had to choose from.

As we made our way through the rows and rows of evergreen trees, we came upon one that we thought would be a perfect fit for our house.

After Jake straightened the tree to a standing position and looked all around it, we all decided that the tree was the one that we wanted and we purchased it.

After Jake had loaded the tree into the back of the truck, we headed back up the dark mountain and toward home. The children were overjoyed with the purchase that we had made and that made me happy to see the children in a cheerful mood. My heart was filling with joy once again.

It was late that night when the tree was finally decorated. I wanted to go out to the front lawn to see how beautiful the house looked at night being decorated with all the lights and tree.

While I stood on the front lawn admiring the decorations, I had an eerie feeling of being watched. As I turned and peered into the woods, I noticed that the lights from the house made the woods too dark to see anything. I tried to overcome the overwhelming feeling that I had and concentrated on the festive decorations.

Being pleased with our work with the decorations, I returned to the porch, took one last look at the front lawn, shut and locked the door, and headed upstairs to retire to my bed.

As to no surprise, the yells and screams that were coming from the woods that night were distracting and terrorizing. As soon as I would doze off to sleep, there would be another frightening scream echo through the forest. Surprisingly, Jake and the children slept soundly. The yells and screams had never woken them from their slumber.

The next morning, I groggily arose to a cold and cloudy day. With the sounds that came from the forest and Jake's snoring, I was in a dour mood, and I knew that I could not go on without sleep for too much longer.

After bathing, I felt better. I headed down to the kitchen and poured a fresh cup of coffee. The children were still asleep in their beds, and I knew I would be able to enjoy my coffee before starting with breakfast.

Jake was up and out of the house early that morning. I knew he had his chores to do and he wanted to get them done early in the day.

As I sat at the kitchen table, I started reading the local newspaper that Jake had brought home the day before.

I was submerged in an interesting article in the newspaper when I suddenly heard Jake walk onto the back porch. As I looked up from my reading material, I noticed he had a strange object in his hands.

I get up and go to the back porch to investigate. I watched as Jake squatted down to inspect the big pile of twisted metal that was lying on the back porch.

"What is that?" I asked when he looked up at me.

"That's all the bear traps that I had put out," Jake said with a confused expression.

"I found them in a pile, and they were thrown into the front yard," Jake said as he looked toward the tree line in the back of the property.

As I looked at the twisted pile of metal that was on the porch in front of Jake, I couldn't believe that was the same traps that he had brought out of the CO-OP a few months ago. They did not look anything like it.

As I was staring at the distorted bear traps, Cody came from behind me and out onto the porch. The children were out of their beds, and I had to put breakfast on the table.

The dark clouds hung lowly, and the cold winds howled on for the rest of the day and into the evening. I was still in a somewhat unhappy mood, but I thought that I would make one of my favorite dishes for dinner and it would help me with the helpless feeling that I had held onto that day.

After dinner, exhausted but happy, we started to relax in the living room in front of the fireplace. Everything was going well until we heard someone or something walk onto the front porch.

With the Christmas tree in the bay window and the wreath on the front door, it was hard to look around them from the inside of the house to see the front porch.

As we waited for a knock on the front door, the heavy footsteps continued. The steps would walk back and forth on the porch, but we never heard a knock.

I started to get nervous. I glanced over at Jake to see what his reaction would be.

As we waited to see if there would be a knock at the door, we suddenly heard a low guttural growl coming from the other side of the front door.

I started to panic. Jake jumped up in a rush to grab his shotgun. He then stood by the door and silently listened for the next movement from out on the porch.

As the children and I huddled on the sofa, I watched every move that Jake made. When we heard the footsteps again, Jake jumped back away from the door and aimed his shotgun toward the front door.

"Who's there?" Jake yelled as he readied his weapon for a shot.

Suddenly, the horrid nightmare became a reality as the creature started banging on the door, trying to get in.

"Get out of here!" Jake yelled at the creature as he kept his aim at the front door.

Between the frightened, crying children, the creature's deafening pounds on the door, and Jake's frantic yells, I felt that the walls were closing in on me as I huddled with Cody and Emma on the sofa.

When I thought the nightmare couldn't have possibly gotten any worse, I heard the loud gun fire followed by the deafening ringing in my ears.

Jake had shot through the front door!

As the ringing in my ears continued, I watched as Jake opened the front door, ran out onto the porch, down the steps, turned toward the barn and disappeared.

While I tried to calm the frightened children, I prayed that Jake would be safe and would come back soon to the safety of the house. I was terrified to be alone even though I knew Jake was outside with the horrifying creature.

Time had passed when I heard Jake walking up the steps and into the house. When he appeared in the doorway, I saw something on his face. I saw that he was very scared.

With his pale skin and his shaking hands, he turned to lock the bullet ridden door. After making sure that the children were well and unharmed, he fell into the chair beside the fireplace.

As he cradled the shotgun in his arms, he sat with wide eyes and stared at the front door as if he expected the monster to come back to terrorize us again.

It was past midnight when Jake had finally started to relax. The children were fast asleep cuddled on the sofa, and my eyes were heavy and needed rest also.

Jake and I took the children up to their rooms and I headed to the master bedroom while Jake went back downstairs to the front room of the house to sleep on the sofa.

The next morning as the sun rose, I went to check on Jake and to make sure the house was still intact. I was surprised to see that Jake was still sitting in his chair while the shotgun rested beside him.

"Did you get any sleep last night?" I asked as I entered the room.

"Just a little" Jake replied as he looked up at me.

"I'll fix a pot of coffee" I replied as I went into the kitchen to brew the coffee and prepare pancakes for breakfast.

Jake and I met in the kitchen and while I was pouring a cup of coffee for myself, Jake reluctantly told me what he encountered the night before.

"There's more than one out there Jada" Jake said as he took a sip of his coffee.

"How do you know that? I asked, knowing that I trusted what he said but didn't want to believe it.

"When I chased after the one that was on the porch, I went toward the barn. When I got closer to the barn and looked out into the fields where the one was running to, I saw three more standing out in the fields." Jake replied.

"I don't like it Jake," I said after he had finished what he was telling me.

"I don't know what to do," Jake said as he took another sip of his coffee.

After feeding the children and cleaning the kitchen of all the breakfast dishes, I needed to talk to Karen. She had a way of calming my nerves more than anyone I knew. And at the time, my nerves were out of control, and I felt that I was losing my mind.

When I disconnected the phone with Karen, I did feel better knowing that I wasn't losing my mind. I had a dear friend to talk to and she understood what I was going through.

We haven't had any visitors from the forest since the last incident that left the front door full of bullet holes. I was feeling a little more relaxed thinking that maybe we had finally scared the creatures away or they had left for the winter.

It was a week before Christmas, and I had not gone shopping for the gifts that had to be under the tree on the day of Christmas. It was time to go to town.

Jake and I loaded the children into the truck and headed down the mountain into town. The holiday festivities were a joy to see and made my heart swell with the Christmas spirit.

After having breakfast at one of our favorite diners in town, it was time to go shopping. Jake and I would take our turn with Cody and Emma while the other one would go get the gifts for them without them knowing it. It was arduous work but I enjoyed every minute of it.

The morning turned to afternoon and the afternoon turned into evening.

Surprisingly, I would find places to stop at even though I knew I would not find anything for the children in the store. Secretly, I was trying to stay in town for as long as I could for I dreaded to go back up into the mountains.

When our shopping money was depleted, and we loaded up on the necessities, we were ready to go home.

As we made our way up the mountain, I realized how quiet and peaceful the drive was. The exhausted children were fast asleep, the cab of the truck was toasty warm, and the hum of the engine made me relaxed and wanted to sleep. I could hardly wait till we were home to retire for the night in my comfortable bed.

As we pulled into the driveway, we headed to the front of the house to unload our cargo.

Jake and I would carry the children in to put them to bed and then unload all the bags from the day's shopping.

I followed Jake up the front porch steps and waited until he unlocked the door to go in.

As soon as I stepped onto the front porch, I started to smell that same putrid smell that we all have smelled before, and my heart started to race.

It wasn't until Jake had opened the door that the smell intensified a hundredfold and I started to be frightened.

As Jake opened the door and I peered into the house, I was appalled by what I saw.

The house had been broken into and the kitchen was destroyed!

I was in shock! As I slowly walked toward the kitchen I noticed that the back door was ripped off and lying on the back porch. The cabinets were all opened, the doors were broken, and the food boxes were ripped and thrown on the floor with the refrigerator was lying on its side. The kitchen was destroyed!

While trying not to breathe in the horrid smell that surrounded me, I felt defeated, and I started to break down and weep.

Jake had put Cody down on the sofa and picked up the shotgun that he left by the fireplace. He then walked out of the front door and turned toward the barn. I went to sit with the children on the sofa and waited until Jake came back.

He had gone to get the tools he needed to replace the back door and to secure the house once again.

As I was helping Jake with the back door, I started to hear screams in the woods. At first, they seemed far off. But as more screams echoed through the woods, the closer they came to the house. I was frightened.

I noticed that Jake was getting nervous every time we would hear the screams coming from the woods. He would stop working on the door and listen as the screams went on. As soon as they would stop, he would hurriedly work on putting the door back in its place.

Once the door was secured in place and locked, Jake and I started to clean the destroyed kitchen.

As I was picking up the ruined food and placing the broken cabinets out of the way, an overwhelming sadness came over me, and tears started rolling down my face once again.

But the tears stopped and was replaced by fear. We could still hear the yells and screams that were coming from the back woods of our property, and they were getting closer.

When the screams were just inside the tree line of our property, Jake decided that he could scare them away with a loud shot from his weapon.

We found out that by shooting the shotgun was a bad idea!

As soon as Jake fired his weapon and came back into the house, all hell broke loose!

There were rocks and trees hitting the house and we both heard a Bigfoot that had climbed on top of the roof trying to get inside the house. The rocks that were being thrown broke the windows of the house, destroying the beautiful Christmas tree and anything that was in the way.

Jake tried to keep the fire in the fireplace roaring while dodging the rocks and firewood that were being thrown through the windows. The weather that night was below freezing, and we were cold.

Jake and I along with the children were trapped in our own home! We hid in our front living room hoping and praying that the creatures would not come into the house and try to kill us. I was terrified!

The attack lasted until daybreak. When the activity had suddenly ceased, we gathered our nerve to go access the damage and to be sure that the many Bigfoot had left.

As we made our way through the destroyed farmhouse, both Jake and I knew that the damage was beyond repair.

The tears welled up in my eyes and at that moment, I knew that our paradise was no more.

"Jake," I said in a trembling voice.

As he turned to look at me and our eyes met, I knew this was it.

We were broken and defeated. It was time to go.

"Pack what you can and put in the truck," Jake said as he turned and walked out the front door and toward the barn.

I frantically started packing the necessities that we truly needed and piled them into the back of the truck on top of the shopping bags and Christmas presents that we had purchased the day before.

After I filled the truck be to the top and couldn't put anything else in the loaded down bed, I gathered the children and put them in the cab and waited for Jake to jump into the driver's seat.

While Jake was getting into the truck I noticed that he threw something on top of all the other stuff that was loaded in the back of the truck. I couldn't tell what it was but at the moment, that was the least of my worries.

As he started the truck and put it in drive, we started rolling forward toward the driveway, I looked back and watched as the farmhouse slowly disappeared and my heart started to sink.

As we neared the main highway to start at the entrance of our driveway, Jake stopped the truck, put it in park and got out and walked around to my side of the truck.

That's when the realization really had sunk in. I noticed what he had in his hand as he started pounding it into the ground. It was the same for-sale sign that we had so proudly taken up when we purchased the property three years ago.
Jake had kept it in the barn when we removed it from the ground.

As I watched Jake pound the post that the for-sale was on into the ground, the tears once again started rolling down my face. I knew it was over. We had lost everything. The farm animals, the house, and the property. We had nothing left.

When Jake returned to the truck, I watched as a tear roll down his cheek, and my broken heart shattered into a million pieces. I knew that his dream was to own a farm in the mountains and I knew that his heart was broken too.

"Are you ready for a new home? Jake asked as he put the truck in drive and pulled out of our driveway.

"Yes, I'm ready" I replied as I wiped the tears off my face.

We drove down the mountain in silence for the last time.

CONCLUSION

It took many years for Jake and I to overcome the terrifying experiences that we went through during our time living in the Appalachian Mountains. We had thought that we would settle there for many years, raise our children and grow old in our little paradise.

It was devastating to lose everything that we worked so hard for, but we were blessed to make it out with our children safely. Material things can be replaced, but life cannot be replaced.

As I mentioned material things. Jake and his father, Arthur, went back up to the farmhouse and packed the remaining items that we had left behind at the house when we left the first time.

We did sell the property to a young couple. They wanted a mountain/vacation retreat. We made sure that the purchasers knew why we had moved out and were selling the property.　　They were skeptic individuals and wanted the property anyway. As they told us, they fell in love with the place, just like we did.

With the damaged farmhouse, we sold the property "as is" with an unbeatable price, lower than the purchase price that was offered to us.

After the move, we decided to go back to my hometown in the state of Florida, where there were flat lands and no mountains in sight. I did miss the small touristy city at the foot of the mountain. I still reminisce about the enjoyable times that Jake and I, with our children, would have in the small town.

While Jake and I wanted our children to grow up in the countryside, learning how to raise their own food and animals, and away from the city life, it didn't work out the way we had planned. But they grew up with other qualities that if living in the country would not have provided.

Through the years as the children were getting older, Cody would sometimes ask me about the farmhouse in the mountains. I was surprised that he remembered us living there. He would tell me what he remembered, and it broke my heart to know that he remembered the good times that we had, and sometimes he would mention the "monster in the woods."

When I asked Emma about if she remembered about living there, she had no recollection of the mountains. I was relieved that she was young enough not to remember what had happened at the property.

As stated earlier, we moved back to my home town located in the state of Florida. Jake and I are now retired and living the good life, surrounded by many loving friends and family.

GALLERY

When I first started writing "Sharing the Mountain with Bigfoot" book series, I wanted to keep readers engaged in the story of our lives and the experiences that we lived through when we lived in the Appalachian Mountains. What better way to do that than with pictures.

I started searching for pictures that I had taken of the property and farmhouse when we lived there, but sadly, with all the effort I had put forth, I could not find one picture of the property.

I know that we all lose personal items throughout our lifetime, but to lose a part of our history that has been haunting us throughout the years, I was dumbfounded.

When I told Jake that I could not find any pictures of us living at the property, he came up with an idea.

Road Trip!

At first, I was hesitant about going back to the mountains and relive the horrors of what had happened there, but that was the only way that I could possibly attain the pictures that I needed. Reluctantly, I agreed to go and visit the place that was once our little paradise in the mountains.

It took us about eleven hours to make it to the small touristy city at the foot of the mountain where we booked a hotel for remainder of our visit.

Being in the small city and visiting the shops and diners that we once frequently visited, my mind was flooded by the memories of the days gone by.

Thank you for reading and if you wish to leave a review, please do for I enjoy reading them.

The driveway to the farmhouse. The potholes are abundant once again.

As Jake and I drove up the mountain toward the property, I started reminiscing about the times that we would travel this road. (Main road up the mountain toward the farmhouse)

The small tourist town. View from the main road up the mountain.

The beautiful river. Since we could not walk back to the river from the property, this view of the river is down from the property but the same river.

When Jake and I drove up the driveway, we were shocked at the condition of the farmhouse. It seemed that it had been abandoned for a while. As I took this picture, my heart was breaking (I took this picture standing where the barn once stood). There was no trace of the barn.

Printed in Great Britain
by Amazon

27849249R00059